Please return / renew this item by last date
shown. Books may be renewed by
telephoning, writing to or calling in at any
library or on the internet.

For Laura and Jonathan. S.G.
For Mum – with love C.F.

ORCHARD BOOKS
96 Leonard Street, London EC2A 4XD
Orchard Books Australia
32/45-51 Huntley Street, Alexandria, NSW 2015
ISBN 1 84362 579 2 (hardback)
ISBN 1 84362 580 6 (paperback)
First published in Great Britain in 2005
First paperback publication in 2006
Text © Susan Gates 2005
Illustrations © Chris Fisher 2005
The rights of Susan Gates to be identified as the author
and of Chris Fisher to be identified as the illustrator of this
work have been asserted by them in accordance with the
Copyright, Designs and Patents Act, 1988.
A CIP catalogue record for this book is available
from the British Library.
1 3 5 7 9 10 8 6 4 2 (hardback)
1 3 5 7 9 10 8 6 4 2 (paperback)
Printed in Great Britain

The
Ice
Thief

SUSAN GATES
Illustrated by Chris Fisher

ORCHARD BOOKS

CHAPTER 1

Gideon crept out of the wood. Fresh snow creaked under his feet. He was dragging a wooden sledge. And carrying an axe over his shoulder.

He stared in shock at the windows of the palace. He was expecting them, like last night, to be shuttered and dark. But now they were blazing with light.

"Drat them," he thought. "They're back."

The Grand Duke had several palaces. This one wasn't his favourite. He thought it was far too small and cramped. It only had twenty-seven bathrooms. He and his family and friends visited it once a year, for the Winter Ball.

Gideon hissed through his teeth, "Trust it to be tonight."

It would make what he had to do far more dangerous.

He was heading for the palace gardens. Usually, they were only lit by moonlight – he could slip through the shadows. But now, in the light glowing from the great windows, they seemed as bright as day.

Icicles, dripping from the fountains, sparkled like the

chandeliers in the ballroom.

"What if somebody sees me?" thought Gideon, hesitating on the edge of the wood.

He was scared. He could end up in chains in a prison cell. But he was more scared of what was waiting for him at home, if he lost his nerve.

"I never saw them arriving," thought Gideon. What had he been doing when the Grand Duke's golden coaches came rumbling through the village? Like all the other villagers he always ran out and cheered and waved his cap.

But today he'd missed them.

"Wonder if Miss Frosty-face came?" he thought.

The Grand Duke was bad enough, with his long snooty hooter. But the Little Duchess, his daughter, was far worse for snootiness. At least the Duke sometimes gave the villagers a stiff little smile back. And once he'd thrown them some pennies. But she had a face like stone. When her coach sped through the village, pulled by six galloping horses, she never even glanced through the windows.

Sometimes she closed the curtains, as if the village and all the people in it didn't interest her one bit.

Gideon shivered at the edge of the wood, trying to get his courage up.

"You can't stay here all night," he told himself.

He'd freeze to death. His feet and hands were wrapped in rags to try and keep out the winter chill. But the cold pierced through the rag bundles, to his bones.

He'd have to risk it.

With his axe and his sledge, Gideon stepped out from the shelter of the wood. He slipped through the small wooden door in the wall that the Head Gardener always forgot to lock. And into the Grand Duke's garden.

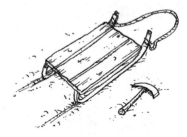

CHAPTER 2

From a window high up in the palace, the Little Duchess looked down on the garden with its frozen ponds and statues hung with icicles.

She yawned and sighed, "There's nothing interesting to look at."

She was about to close the curtains. Then she saw something fluttering down there. It looked like a big wounded bird. It was shuffling along the snowy paths.

"What's that?" thought the Little Duchess, leaning closer to the window.

Then she saw it wasn't a wounded bird. It was a peasant person, trailing rags, not feathers.

"What cheek," thought the Little Duchess. "It should go to the back door."

Peasants weren't allowed at the front.

Then she thought, "What's it doing here, anyway?" The rag bundle was creeping towards the biggest pond, a huge marble basin. Round the rim were twenty-two stone mermaids, combing their long hair.

The rag bundle stopped by the mermaid pond. It seemed to be staring round, as if it was scared of being caught.

The Little Duchess yawned again. She wasn't all that curious. She hardly got curious or excited about anything. But, for some reason, she kept on watching.

Gideon felt sick. He could hear the jerky beat of his own heart. He could already feel those chains, round his wrists and ankles. This was far too risky.

"Quickly, quickly," he told himself. "Don't hang about."

He was so close to the palace now, he could see people dancing. Their shadows capered on walls and ceilings. He could see fiddlers fiddling away like mad, their faces red and sweaty from the heat of a thousand candles.

Then he saw something else.

On tables, piled high with food, there were fantastic ice-cream puddings.
Some were
s h a p e d
like swans,
like castles!
And round

each pudding, to keep it from melting, were great heaps of ice.

"That's my ice," said Gideon proudly.

It glittered in the light like diamonds.

"The finest ice in the world," whispered Gideon, forgetting for a second how scared he was.

And it came from the Grand Duke's own marble ponds. Gideon couldn't help grinning about that. He was an ice thief. In winter, he stole ice from ponds and sold it to cooks in grand houses, so they could make ice-cream puddings for parties.

Last night he'd knocked at the back door of the palace and sold a great sparkling sledgeful of ice to the cook. She'd come here a week early to prepare the Winter Ball Banquet.

Gideon had to stuff a hand over his mouth to stop himself laughing out loud. It was a brilliant joke. Selling the Grand Duke's own ice to the Grand Duke's cook.

"That cook!" Gideon thought, shaking his head. "She'd probably pay

good money for her own piddle!"

Would he try to sell her some more ice tonight?

Gideon frowned to himself. "It's too dangerous." Last night

there was no one about. Since then, the palace had filled up – with servants, guests and guards. It was swarming with people!

But the Grand Duke's cook paid a good price. Better than any of the other cooks round here. And, if Gideon went home with a purse full of money, it might put Pa in a good mood.

Gideon shivered. Not from the cold this time, but because he was thinking about Pa. He tried to block Pa out of his mind. It wasn't good for his concentration.

He tore his dazzled gaze away from the ballroom. From the tables piled high with roast chickens and puddings.

They had made him feel hungry. There was an icicle dripping from the nose of a stone mermaid. He reached up, snapped it off and crunched it.

It didn't stop his belly rumbling.

In her high window, the Little Duchess surprised herself. She actually felt curious. She wanted to know something. She thought: "I wonder what an icicle tastes like?"

Gideon told himself, "Quickly, quickly. You've wasted enough time!" Those palace guards had pikes and muskets.

He stuck his axe in his belt. Then he climbed over the rim of the marble basin.

"He'll drown!" thought the Little Duchess. She didn't realise the pond was frozen. She hardly ever went outside. She didn't understand about ice.

But the boy didn't drown.

Instead, he

skated across the pond on his rag shoes. His hair and tatty clothes fluttered behind him. He swooped like a bird, his arms spread out like wings.

"I wonder what that feels like?" thought the Little Duchess. Just for a moment, she felt a strange longing in her heart.

Gideon was at the centre of the pond now. He brushed away the fresh, feathery snow and peered down. The pond was all ice, right down to the bottom of the marble basin. And there was no mud in it. No green weedy bits or dead leaves, or frozen frogs.

It was clear as crystal, the finest purest ice. Just the kind that cooks would pay a high price for.

Gideon lifted his axe. *Whack,* he split the ice. Chopped out a great lump. Sent it whizzing to the side of the pond.

Scared, he looked round. In the silent garden the splintering ice cracked like gunfire. Surely someone had heard? Surely someone had spotted him? Any second he expected a cry – "Stop, thief!"

But they were all busy dancing. And above the blazing ballroom windows the rest of the palace seemed dark.

Gideon had no idea about the watcher at the high window.

"Quickly, quickly," he murmured, gliding back to the side.

He chopped again with the axe. More urgently this time. He tapped the ice into chunks, and piled it onto his sledge. His fingers poked through the rags. They stung so badly that he had to fight back tears.

Above him, the Little Duchess sat up stiffly in her chair. She'd stopped wondering about skating and what icicles tasted like.

She thought, "He's stealing our ice. What a cheek."

Should she call the guard? Have him arrested?

But then, behind her, a door slammed. The Little Duchess's back stiffened even more. She felt her skin prickle. She sat up very straight in her chair.

"Why are you staring through the window?" asked a haughty voice, cold as the stone mermaids' noses. "You can learn nothing from outside. Outside is for peasants and common people."

It was the Grand Duke's sister, the Arch Duchess. She had never liked the Little Duchess. She found her bothersome, a pain in the neck. It would have been different if the Little Duchess was pretty. But she was a very plain child, in the Arch Duchess's opinion. She took after her mother.

"It was by going outside that your mother died," the Arch Duchess reminded her. "If she hadn't kissed that dribbling peasant child, doubtless she wouldn't have died of that dreadful disease. But she was always doing things like that. Being friendly to servants and common people. Most unsuitable!"

Every chance she got, the Arch Duchess said rude things about the Little Duchess's mother.

The Little Duchess felt her lip quivering. She was nine now. Her mother had died when she was a baby. The Arch Duchess always said, "You can't possibly remember her! You were too little!" And the Little Duchess always insisted fiercely, "Yes, I do!"

Her memories were hazy – but as comforting as a hot-water bottle. They were of warm cuddles and kind smiles and lullabies, whose words she could never remember, sung over her cradle.

The Arch Duchess was dressed for the ball. She had only dropped in for a minute. The Little Duchess saw her aunt every day. She saw the Grand Duke, her father, on birthdays and at Christmas. And sometimes, in the distance, down a long corridor, surrounded by important people.

The Arch Duchess showed her teeth, in a chilly smile. "You may kiss me before I go," she said, as if it was a great favour.

She was loaded down with jewellery. She jangled when she walked. She had a wig on, like a wobbly white meringue. She had eyes like a weasel and a mean, pouty mouth.

The Little Duchess screwed her eyes tight shut. She aimed a peck at the Arch Duchess's powdery cheek.

"Don't spoil my make-up," snapped the Arch Duchess. "You clumsy child. You take after your mother. She was always clumsy."

She jangled out of the room. Then stuck her wig back round the door.

"You should learn from the friend I found you," she told the Little Duchess. "She'll show you how a proper Duchess ought to behave."

As soon as the Arch Duchess had gone, the Little Duchess peered out of the window again. The ice thief was gone. She couldn't see him anywhere in the frozen garden. Perhaps the guards had got him. She felt a tiny twinge of regret.

But then she set her face like stone. Put on her haughty look. "Serve him right," she thought.

The friend the Arch Duchess had found her had been sitting quiet on a golden stool all this time. The Little Duchess turned to her. "Shall we play the flute together?" she said, sighing.

CHAPTER 3

Gideon hadn't been arrested. Not yet. He was dragging his sledge, loaded with glittering ice, round the side of the palace.

He had to make a decision. Should he sell the Grand Duke his own ice? Did he dare? Or should he drag his sledge to Howton Hall, half a mile down the road?

"The Grand Duke's cook pays twice the price," thought Gideon.

And Pa would be very pleased about that. It would put him in a good mood – for a while.

That was worth any risk. Gideon laid his axe on the sledge, next to his sparkling treasure. He took a deep breath. And trudged off to the kitchen door.

The stable yard was dark. Was there anyone about? Only the horses, snorting and stamping in the stables.

Their breath floated out in frosty plumes.

The sledge bumped on the cobblestones.

"Shhh!" Gideon warned himself. He stopped to listen, his heart hammering. But no one shouted, "Hey, you!" All the servants must be busy at the ball.

Gideon swallowed hard. He still had time to sneak away, sell his ice at Howton Hall. "If you get caught," he murmured, "they'll put you in chains. It'll be a prison cell for you."

But then he imagined Pa in a good mood. And the kitchen door was just over there. Behind it was the cook, her fat arms all floury.

"What are you waiting for?" Gideon asked himself.

He gave himself a good shake. Then strode up to the kitchen door, rapped softly on it with his axe handle.

Rat-tat-tat-tat-tat. Silence. No one came. But then the door creaked open. A pale, ratty face peeped out. And in one awful second Gideon saw it wasn't the cook. The door was flung open now. It was the most junior footman, a boy about his age, in a fancy jacket and tight white trousers.

He took one look at Gideon. "Help!" he shrieked. "It's a murderer! He's got an axe!" He fled out into the night, screaming, "Guards!"

Gideon panicked, and threw down the axe. He couldn't go back through the stable yard. That was the way the guards would come. Any second now, they'd be clanking over the cobblestones. Like a trapped animal, he dodged through the door, and bolted across the kitchen.

The cook saw him, stopped stirring custard, and opened her mouth in shock.

But the boy was already gone.

Gideon was inside the palace. But he didn't even think about that. His only thought was, "Escape! Escape!" He panted up stone steps, down dark narrow corridors. Flung himself

through big double doors. The corridors changed. He was out of the servants' quarters now, running on  carpets, past golden chairs and precious Ming vases. But he didn't notice the difference. His mind was whirling. Everything around him was just a blur.

"Climb! Climb!" he panted to himself. As if the higher he climbed, the safer he would be.

He staggered up another staircase. Then doubled up, gasping. A stitch burned like fire in his side. But could that be guards clanking behind him?

Mad with terror, Gideon hurled himself through the nearest door.

He was sprawled on a soft carpet.

Slowly, the world stopped whirling. He could hear the sound of a flute playing. Still panting, Gideon lifted his head.

It was the Little Duchess! She had her back to him, playing her flute, but you couldn't mistake her. No other child dressed like her. Not like a little girl but like a grand lady. With a high, white wig and rich gown stiff with jewels and embroidery.

"Run away!" Gideon's brain told him. "Do it now. Before she sees you!"

But the flute music bewitched him. It was so lovely, so soothing.

"Like angels' voices," thought Gideon, as he found himself on his feet and tiptoeing closer. He just couldn't help it. "I'll just stay a second longer," he told himself.

Still, the Little Duchess hadn't noticed. She sat up stiff and straight on her golden stool, with her back to him. Staring out the window, playing her flute. As if Gideon didn't exist.

Gideon was very close now. Practically breathing down her neck. Still she didn't turn round.

He stretched out his hand. His brain told him, "This is madness." But he wanted to make her notice him. To tell her, "That's the most beautiful music I ever heard."

He touched her on the neck.

Instantly, a little door in her neck flew open.

"Aaargh!" yelled Gideon, staggering back.

Inside the Little Duchess there were cogs and wheels, pulleys and wires. The wires were twanging, her wheels whizzing round...

Gideon felt hot and dizzy, as if he was about to faint.

At that moment another Little Duchess came out of the next room, carrying the flute she'd been looking for.

Gideon looked wildly from one to another. He just couldn't work it out. He'd walked straight into a nightmare!

CHAPTER 4

The real Little Duchess recognised him at once. He was the ragged boy she'd seen eating icicles, skimming like a bird over the pond, stealing the Grand Duke's ice.

"Don't be alarmed," she said, calmly. "I am the real Little Duchess. And this is my friend, the Clockwork Duchess."

Still, Gideon struggled to take it in. They seemed identical – the same stiff, jewelled frocks, the same wigs, the same haughty look.

"She is mechanical," explained the Little Duchess. She was thinking, "Is this peasant boy foolish? It's all quite simple."

The Arch Duchess had ordered a doll maker to make the Clockwork Duchess. She didn't approve of the Little Duchess mixing with other children. None of them were grand enough; they might teach her bad manners. Worse still, she might even like them, as her mother had done. And that would be most unduchesslike. No, a clockwork duchess was the ideal companion.

"Say hello, Clockwork Duchess," ordered the Little Duchess.

The Clockwork Duchess swivelled round on her stool. *Whirr, clank.* Bellows started up somewhere inside her. They puffed air through her lips. She made sounds!

"Charmed, I'm sure," said the Clockwork Duchess, in a strange, wheezy voice.

Gideon forgot he was on the run. That the palace guards might catch up with him any minute. He shuffled forward on his rag-bound feet.

"It's magic!" he said.

"No, it isn't," said the Little Duchess firmly.

"She looks just like you!"

"No, she doesn't," said the Little Duchess.

Now Gideon looked closer, he could see that she was right. The Clockwork Duchess wasn't like the real Duchess. She had creamy skin without a single mole or pimple. She didn't have freckles, like the real Duchess. She had a much cuter nose and her lips were as red as cherries. The Arch Duchess had ordered her made like that. "It's an improvement on the real thing," she'd told the doll maker. "And much less of a nuisance."

The Clockwork Duchess did just what you told her. She never complained. She only ever said, "Charmed, I'm sure." She was much prettier. She never, ever did anything unduchesslike. The Arch Duchess much preferred her to her real, live niece.

"I hate her," the Little Duchess told Gideon, giving the Clockwork Duchess's tin legs a kick. "She's just too perfect. And she plays the flute much better than me."

Gideon pulled off his tatty cap. seemed to have lost his tongue. He blushed and stammered. He'd suddenly realised he was in terrible trouble. He'd just burst into the private rooms of the Grand Duke's daughter! If you got chucked into jail for stealing ice, what would be his punishment for this?

"Don't give me away," he pleaded, backing towards the door. "I'm going now."

"You're an ice thief," said the Little Duchess, coldly. "I saw you. You stole it from the mermaid pond."

"Charmed, I'm sure," wheezed the Clockwork Duchess, like a set of leaky bagpipes.

"Shut up," snapped the Little Duchess. "I'm talking."

Gideon groaned. So she'd seen him! He was in even more trouble than he'd thought. "I won't do it again," he said. "Honest."

"What do you do with my father's ice?" asked the Little Duchess in her snootiest voice. "After you steal it?"

"I sell it," confessed Gideon "to your father's cook."

He could have kicked himself. He thought, "What did you tell her that for? Now you're for it!"

The Little Duchess gave him that frosty glare. As if he was something nasty she'd trodden in.

But then a strange thing happened. Her stone face seemed to crack up. A strange, whooping sound came from her mouth.

Gideon thought, amazed, "She's laughing."

She was laughing so hard she had to hug her belly.

"Stop. You'll hurt yourself," said Gideon.

The Little Duchess wiped tears from her eyes. She'd never laughed so much in her life. "What a good joke," said the Little Duchess, still giggling.

"That's what I thought," agreed Gideon.

"What's your name, boy?" asked the Little Duchess.

Gideon drew himself up. He puffed out his chest. "I am the Ice King," he said.

The Little Duchess's voice became frosty again. "You are not the King. I have seen the King."

"That's what they call me round here," boasted Gideon. "Because I know all the best ice ponds. I can get ice from places others daren't go."

"Steal it, you mean," the Little Duchess reminded him.

Gideon backed towards the door. "She's getting snooty again," he warned himself. For a moment, he'd thought everyone was wrong about her. That she wasn't really Miss High-and-Mighty but a friendly sort of girl you could share a joke with.

Gideon shuffled back a bit more, while the Little Duchess glared at him. Was she going to call the guard?

Suddenly, the Clockwork Duchess butted in. "Charmed, I'm—" Then she stopped. Her voice became low and growly. "Sssssuuuure," she said, and then slumped forward. Her wig fell off.

It rolled across the floor. And behind her beautiful porcelain face, Gideon could see her head, as bald and shiny as a tin egg.

He shuddered.

"I'm not going to wind her up again," said the Little Duchess.

And Gideon found himself saying, "I don't blame you. She gives me the creeps."

There was an awkward silence.

Gideon said, "They don't really call me the Ice King. I just made that up. Gideon's my real name."

Rat-tat-tat-tat-tat.

Gideon and the Little Duchess almost jumped out of their skin.

"There's someone at the door," said Gideon, his scared eyes like saucers.

"Leave this to me." The Little Duchess swept past him.

"Who knocks?" she called out in her chilliest tones.

"It's me, the cook, milady," hissed a voice through the door.

"The cook! Don't open the door!" gabbled Gideon.

"Don't be foolish," said the Little Duchess. "The cook is only a servant."

She opened the door, just a crack. But the cook burst through. She looked hot and puffed out from climbing so many stairs.

"I've found you at last!" she said to Gideon.

"What is the meaning of this, Cook?" said the Little Duchess, sternly. "I know he stole ice from our mermaid pond. But he won't do it again."

"What did you tell her that for?" groaned Gideon. "She didn't know where I got it from."

"Of course I did," said the cook. "Do you think I've got mashed potato for brains? But I saw you were a poor, ragged child. And I thought, 'He could do with the money.'"

Gideon gawped at her.

"But anyway," said the Cook, "I've come to warn you. The guards are coming this way."

"I've got to hide!" said Gideon, panicking all over again.

"No," said the cook. "They'll find you. Even here. I'll show you a secret way out, through the cellars."

"Let's go, then," said Gideon. "Quick! Quick!" He could already feel those guards grabbing his collar.

"I'm coming too," said the Little Duchess, suddenly.

They both turned to stare at her.

"No, milady," said the cook. "You'll get your fine dress all dirty. You'll be missed."

"No, I won't," said the Little Duchess. "Help me."

She struggled to sit the Clockwork Duchess up straight. *Clank, clank.*

"That doll needs oiling," said the cook.

"Never mind that now. Help me wind her up!"

The Little Duchess unbuttoned the back of the doll's dress. Got a big key out of a drawer. "It's hard to turn."

But the cook had strong fingers from squeezing lemons. And arms like a wrestler from pastry rolling. She clicked the key round in the doll's back. As she did, the Clockwork Duchess jerked up. Her tin head glittered in the light.

"Her wig!" said the cook.

Gideon ran to get it, plonked it on the clockwork doll's head. It was skew-whiff but no one would notice.

The Little Duchess put the flute in her fingers. *Whirr, click,* those wheels started turning. The Clockwork Duchess raised the flute to her lips.

"Hurry!" pleaded the cook. She picked up a fat white candle with the biggest flame. "We'll need this where we're going," she said.

The Little Duchess did one last thing. She blew out the other candles. "They'll never see the difference in the dark," she said. "They'll think it's me."

"Wait!" said Gideon, dashing back. He shut the little door on the Clockwork Duchess's neck. It made him shudder to do it. But it was a dead give-away – being able to see all those cogs and wheels whirring inside her.

He dashed outside again. They raced down the long corridor with the cook puffing and panting in front of them

"This way!" The cook suddenly plunged behind red velvet curtains, through a tiny door.

"I never knew that was there," thought the Little Duchess.

Behind them, in the moonlit room, the Clockwork Duchess played on. She was on her own. But she didn't feel lonely or sad. She didn't feel anything. She was just mechanical. Her perfect, cornflower-blue eyes gazed out at nothing at all.

CHAPTER 5

"Down here," gasped the cook.

They stumbled down winding stairs with the cook's candle lighting the way. Down and down, then through a maze of tunnels.

"Aaargh!"

Gideon trod on something squishy. It flopped away into the dark.

"A toad," said the cook over her shoulder. "All sorts of creatures live down here. Bats, toads, rats—"

The Little Duchess gave a quick shudder. Rats! She'd just seen a pair of red, glowing eyes watching them through the darkness.

"There's a yellow rope along the wall," said the cook.

"I can feel it," said the Little Duchess, grasping the scratchy rope like a lifeline.

"Just keep hold of that," said the cook, "and it'll guide you, even in the dark."

They were in the cellars now, great brick caves with dusty wine bottles and wooden barrels.

Moonlight came splashing in through a small iron grille. "This is the way out," said the cook. She forced back a rusty bolt. The grille swung open.

"Goodbye, boy," she said to Gideon.

"Come on, milady," she said to the Little Duchess. "We'd better get back or my custard will curdle."

The Little Duchess said, "I'm going with Gideon."

"What?" said the cook flustered. "No, no, milady, you must come back with me."

 The Little Duchess's voice was extra haughty. But this time she meant it to be. "Cook, do not be disobedient!" But then she added, "If I'm with Gideon he will come to no harm. The guards won't dare touch him."

"I'll be all right on my own," said Gideon.

"I will see you safely on your way," insisted the Little Duchess. "Then I shall come back to the palace."

The cook and Gideon looked at each other. The Little Duchess's face had that, *Don't-argue-with-me* look.

The cook sighed. "As you wish, milady." Still, the cook lingered. The Little Duchess knew nothing about the big, wide world. She'd hardly ever been outside the palace walls.

But the Little Duchess had already crawled through the tiny grille where the cook was too fat to follow. A small, white face peered back through the ferns. "Go!" it commanded the cook.

Cook bustled off, muttering, into the darkness.

"You shouldn't be so rude to people," said Gideon, as he crawled out after her.

But the Little Duchess wasn't listening. She stood up and shook the snow off her frock. "Where are we?" she asked.

She looked round. Great, tangled trees loomed over them. Somewhere, an owl screeched.

"This is a wild place," said the Little Duchess, suddenly shivering.

"It's only the wood," said Gideon. "Outside the palace walls."

"Outside the walls?" said the Little Duchess.

Gideon could hear that her voice was trembling. "It's all right, I'm safe now," he told her. "You can go back home."

But the Little Duchess had just noticed the blue bruises along Gideon's cheekbones. "Where did you get those?" she asked him. "Did you fall on the ice?"

Gideon shuddered, as if at a bad memory. But all he said was, "I never fall on the ice."

"I saw you sliding," said the Little

Duchess. "On the mermaid pond. It seemed like—" She stopped. She didn't know what word to use.

"Fun?" suggested Gideon. "Look, you'd better go back now."

"Not through those tunnels," shuddered the Little Duchess. There was a rope to guide her. But what about the rustlings, the red eyes in the darkness?

"You don't have to," said Gideon. "You're the Little Duchess, remember. The guards won't arrest you. Just walk along by the wall. And then through the big iron gates. It's easy."

The Little Duchess hesitated. She should go back. She shouldn't be outside the walls, with ragged boys. It was most unduchesslike. But then she thought about what waited for her, back home. Her father, the Grand Duke, whom she saw mostly in the distance. The Arch Duchess with her mean, pouty mouth and vindictive ways. The Clockwork Duchess, who was just too perfect and probably the most useless friend any girl ever had.

"I know I must go back," sighed the Little Duchess to herself. "But not for a little while.

"I want to go ice sliding," she said.

Gideon looked shocked. "Duchesses don't go ice sliding. It's dangerous."

"But I want to," said the Little Duchess, stamping her silver slippers.

Gideon frowned. He said, "All right. Just a quick slide. Come this way."

The Little Duchess followed the ragged boy through the wood. Her high wig kept getting caught on the branches. Her stiff jewelled frock was hard to walk in. But she felt a strange new feeling fizzing inside her. Could it possibly be excitement?

They stepped out of the trees. What looked like a great mirror lay before them. It gleamed silver in the

moonlight. It seemed to stretch for miles.

"It's a meadow," explained Gideon. "That flooded – and then froze."

The Little Duchess felt a great joyfulness sweep over her. She wanted to swoop over the ice field, fly free as a bird. She took off her heavy wig. Then she struggled out of her stiff frock – usually she had two maids standing on stools to lift it off over her head.

Underneath she had layers and layers of white petticoats and vests, but she still felt light as a feather.

"Wheee!" she flung her arms wide, like wings, and launched herself, out onto the ice.

"No!" Gideon shouted. "It's dangerous! Wait for me!" He pushed himself out onto the ice and went swooping after her on his rag-bundled feet.

The Little Duchess felt her face tingling. Her feet were icy-cold in her thin slippers. But she didn't care. The world raced past her in a silvery blur. The wind made a rushing sound in her ears. She had never, in her whole life, felt so alive.

"I'm flying! I'm flying!" she screamed.

For ages in the moonlight, they skated, swooped and twirled.

Gideon almost pinched himself. He couldn't believe it. "She's good fun," he thought, amazed. "Not snooty at all."

She was tough too. She fell over lots of times, her knees were scraped and bleeding. But she just laughed and skated on.

"Hey!" shouted Gideon, as they were gliding past each other. "Have you got another name? Besides the Little Duchess?"

The Little Duchess had to think for a second. She'd almost forgotten.

"My name is Alice," she said, swooping off across the ice.

At last, Alice started shivering. Her teeth were chattering.

"You'd better go home," said Gideon.

"Just one more slide," begged Alice.

Then, through the trees, they heard the rumbling of coaches, the shouts of coachmen: "Whoa there!"

"It's the ball," said Alice. "It's over. The guests are leaving. Perhaps I'd better get back."

She dived into her dress, crammed her wig back on her head. She was the Little Duchess again.

Gideon watched her flitting through the trees. He sighed. That was that then. She'd gone.

"Did you really think," he mocked himself, "that you could be friends?"

Gideon trudged towards home. It had suddenly hit him. He had no money to give to Pa. He'd left behind his sledge and his axe. It made him cringe, just thinking about it.

"You're for it now," he told himself in a tiny, scared whisper.

CHAPTER 6

Alice hurried past the mermaid pond. There was still a crowd of guests leaving. No one noticed her in the crush. She reached up and snapped an icicle from a mermaid's nose. She crunched off a bit.

"Icicles don't taste like anything," she decided as she slipped into the palace.

High above her, the Clockwork Duchess was still playing. Her cornflower-blue eyes stared out at nothing. Suddenly, the twittering flute notes became low and wheezy. Like a cow coughing. Then they stopped altogether. The Clockwork Duchess slumped forwards, her tin arms dangling. She'd run down again.

At that moment, the Arch Duchess jangled through the door. She was in a bad mood, because no one had asked her to dance – well, only the Grand Duke's Personal Assistant, who looked like a toad. She wanted to take it out on the Little Duchess.

She saw a figure in the gloom. She started nagging straightaway.

"Have you put lemon juice on those freckles?"

In her opinion, only common people had freckles. "You get them from your mother," she told the Little Duchess. "Not from our side of the family."

"And why aren't you in bed?" she snapped.

"Clank," said the figure, flopping so far forwards that its forehead clanged off the floor.

"Wait a minute," thought the Arch Duchess.

She wasn't very bright. But even she guessed that she was nagging the Clockwork Duchess instead of the real thing.

Her face screwed up in suspicion. She glanced into the other room. No one there.

"Where is the little brat?" she asked herself.

She hoped that the Little Duchess was doing something wrong. The Arch Duchess was always looking for reasons to be spiteful to her niece. To run with tales about her to her father, the Grand Duke. Though it could be frustrating. Because even when the Arch Duchess said, "Brother! You'll never guess what your daughter has done now!" the Grand Duke would only say, vaguely, "Daughter? What daughter?"

The Arch Duchess stepped outside the door. Just in time to catch Alice trying to sneak back through it.

The Little Duchess's wig was all

frizzy and full of twigs. Her expensive frock was ripped, her embroidered slippers ruined. And she was eating an icicle.

The Arch Duchess couldn't believe her luck. Her small,

weasel eyes glittered.

"Help, help!" she cried dramatically, sliding down the wall. "She has given me such a shock. I am fainting!"

There was a clattering sound as servants rushed up the stairs to help her.

"Have you seen the state of that!" shrieked the Arch Duchess as soon as she had a big enough audience. She pointed a quivering finger. "Does that look like a Duchess to you? No, it doesn't! It looks like any common village girl!"

The Little Duchess stood there, looking defiant, while her icicle melted between her fingers and dripped on to the carpet.

69

"You can expect to be punished for this, my girl," said the Arch Duchess. "Most severely!"

Her weasly face looked grave. But, behind her hand, she hid a sly, gleeful smile.

CHAPTER 7

Gideon decided, "Pa's in bed." He breathed a deep sigh of relief. It wouldn't be as bad as he thought.

The cottage was in darkness. No firelight gleamed through the chinks in the mud walls.

Spiders' webs and great swags of ivy hung down from the thatch. Gideon had to duck under them to get through the door.

He tiptoed in. The last thing he

wanted was to wake Pa. He heard snoring. Good. That meant Pa was sound asleep.

He was starving. His hand groped around on the table, trying to find a crust of bread. Was that one?

"Aaargh!" A vice-like hand gripped his wrist.

A great, red monster face lunged at him across the table. Its mouth opened. A roaring voice deafened him.

"Pa!" gasped Gideon.

"Thought I was asleep, did you, boy?" bellowed Pa. "I been waiting up for you for hours. Where's my beer money?"

Gideon tried to wriggle out of Pa's grip. But Pa was too strong. "Don't get mad, Pa," pleaded Gideon. "But I ain't got none. I—"

But Pa didn't want to listen to excuses. He gave another bellow, like

an angry bull. And whacked his free hand across Gideon's face.

"Pa, don't!" begged Gideon. "Don't beat me."

But Pa was in a red rage. He wanted to take it out on someone. "I've been waiting here all night! Where've you been?"

He raised his hand again. But this time Gideon twisted out of his grip and ran.

"Come back here, boy!" yelled Pa. "I won't hurt you."

But Gideon knew that was a lie. He went crashing through the woods. Branches dumped snow on him, briars tripped him up. At last he crouched under a tree, sobbing. He rubbed his aching wrist, his stinging cheek.

He daren't go back, not without Pa's beer money.

He should go back to the palace,

find his axe and sledge and steal some more ice. Never mind the danger. Never mind if there were guards looking for him. As long as Pa stopped being angry with him.

Gideon tried to stagger up. But he was weary, right through to his bones. His head was fuzzy.

There was a sort of den under the tree's roots, dug out long ago by an animal.

Gideon crawled inside it. It was dry
and snug. He curled up like a stray dog
and tried to sleep.

CHAPTER 8

Alice had woken up very early. She was staring out of her window.

But she wasn't looking at the garden. She was trying to see over the walls, to where the wood was and the frozen meadow. She longed to go ice-sliding again, fly free as a bird.

But she couldn't even go out of her room. She'd been locked in, by the Arch Duchess, as punishment for "most unduchesslike behaviour".

She sighed and tore her gaze away from the window.

She was so lonely she almost wound up the Clockwork Duchess, just to hear another voice. Even if it was a wheezy, mechanical one that only said, "Charmed, I'm sure."

Alice sighed again. She was so restless. She hardly knew what to do with herself. She wandered back to the window. Looked out again.

Through the mist came a shuffling figure, its rags trailing behind it like octopus tentacles.

"Gideon!" thought Alice. "What's he doing here?" Had he come to steal ice again?

Alice banged on the window. "No! Go back. You'll get caught!"

She struggled to open the window, but it was sealed up. No fresh air could get in, in case the Little Duchess caught a chill.

Down in the palace garden, Gideon dodged from hedge to hedge. He couldn't hear Alice's frantic knocking. Her window was too high up.

"You shouldn't be here," Gideon kept telling himself. "Not in daylight." But still he trudged on.

He patted the fresh bruises on his face. He daren't go home without Pa's money. And this might be his last chance. The sun was already softening the ice. Drip, drip, drip, drip. That was the icicles thawing on the mermaids' noses. Soon the pond would start melting.

First, though, he had to find his axe and sledge.

"Please, please," he wished, "let them be where I left them, outside the kitchen door."

"Grrrrr!" Gideon spun round. What was that? Had they seen him? Had they let loose the dogs?

"Look up here! Look up here!" begged Alice behind the thick glass. But Gideon didn't look up.

He crept over the cobblestones of the stable yard.

"Oh no!" Gideon had to clamp a hand over his mouth, to stop himself crying out. His axe and sledge were gone. Someone had taken them from outside the kitchen door.

And suddenly Gideon was hit by a wave of despair. He felt like wailing like a tiny baby.

"What am I going to do now?" he thought.

"Pssst!" A brawny arm shot out of the kitchen door, dragged him inside.

"Ahhh!" yelled Gideon, kicking and struggling. They had got him!

"Will you stop that?" said the cook, dumping him on the stone floor. "Someone will hear you! You look hungry, boy," said the cook, looking at his pinched white face. Her sharp eyes spotted the fresh bruises. But she didn't say anything.

She sawed him off a hunk of fresh-baked, fluffy bread. Gideon crammed it into his mouth with both hands, wolfed down slice after slice.

He felt bolder now his belly was full. The terrible despair was lifting.

"I came for my sledge," he explained. "And my axe. And by the way," he added awkwardly. "I never said thank you."

"What for?" asked the cook.

"For helping me escape last night. For showing me the way out."

The cook shrugged, as if it was nothing.

"Are you thieving ice again?" she asked, as she knocked seven bells out of some bread dough.

Gideon shuffled his feet in embarrassment: "Errrr..."

"Is it for that no-good, drunken pa of yours?" she asked him.

"How do you know about my pa?" said Gideon, squirming.

"You'd be amazed what cooks know," said the cook.

She pursed her lips and didn't say another word about Gideon's pa. But she gave that dough an extra good pummelling.

"The Little Duchess got home safe last night," said the cook.

"Oh, good," said Gideon. "I was worrying."

"Well, she's all right," said the cook. "Except old Prune-face has locked her in her room."

"Old Prune-face?"

"That's what I calls that Arch Duchess," said the cook. "As well as some other names, not fit for children's ears. She's as poisonous as a snake that one. And when I think what a lovely lady the Little Duchess's ma was. Had a kind word for everyone..."

"Her ma?" asked Gideon, mystified.

"What happened to her ma?"

"She died," said the cook, shaking her head sadly.

"That's what happened to my ma," said Gideon, amazed that he had something in common with the Little Duchess besides ice-sliding. "She got a fever. Right after I was born. I don't remember her or nothing."

But, just like the Little Duchess, he often felt an aching inside him and a great, empty, Ma-shaped hole...

"Wait a minute!" roared Gideon, as if he'd suddenly realised something. "Did you just say the Little Duchess was locked up? Is it 'cos she went ice sliding? That's not a crime! That's what children do! And besides, she had fun! She was laughing!"

"Shhh," said the cook. "Calm down. Someone will hear you. Old Prune-face is always prowling around, checking up on servants."

"I don't care!" said Gideon, dashing
out of the kitchen.
"I'm going to talk
to Alice."

"No," said
the cook. "No
one's allowed
to talk to her."

She didn't add,
"especially a ragged ice

thief who calls her Alice, instead of
milady". The Arch Duchess would have
hysterics. She would shriek, "What
disrespect! Lock the boy in the deepest
dungeon! And throw away the key!"

But Gideon had already
disappeared. The cook went huffing
and puffing after him up flights of
stone steps. She caught him up on a
landing where he was staring round,
bewildered. He'd forgotten the way.

"Come back," begged the cook. "You'll get into trouble."

"No," said Gideon, setting his mouth in a stubborn line.

The cook sighed. She thought, "My bread's burning. I must be mad doing this." But she felt sorry for both children. They had no one to care about them. No one on their side. Except for her.

"Right," she said. "I'll show you up there. And I'll keep watch. But only for a few minutes, mind. And then you have to go. Promise!"

But he was already dashing off, not waiting for her.

The cook grabbed him. "Not that way," she hissed. She hustled him up some secret stairs that only servants knew about.

Alice was pacing about her room. She felt sick with worry. Where was Gideon?

"Please don't let the Arch Duchess catch him," she thought.

The cook poked her head from behind a blue Ming vase. "No sign of old Prune-face," she whispered. They tiptoed out.

"That's the door to the Little Duchess's room," whispered the cook.

There was a great iron key in the lock.

"Only five minutes," the cook warned Gideon. "And if I whistle like this," the cook put two fingers in her mouth and gave an ear-splitting blast, "you come running out. Double quick!"

"I promise," said Gideon. But he

wasn't really listening. He was too busy trying to twist the key in the lock.

Alice heard the key rattling. She thought, "It's the Arch Duchess!" She'd been in here twice this morning, trying to catch her doing something unduchesslike. Last time she'd snapped, "Wind up the Clockwork Duchess. She has perfect manners!"

Now, Alice sprang to the Clockwork Duchess and set her going. She didn't want to give the Arch Duchess an excuse to be even more spiteful.

Clank...Whirr. The Clockwork Duchess got up jerkily from her stool.

"Allow me," said the cook to Gideon. "Or we'll be here all day." She barged him aside. Then wrenched the door key round with her strong lemon-squeezing fingers.

"Five minutes!" she hissed, diving behind some curtains. Gideon slipped inside the Little Duchess's room.

CHAPTER 9

"Gideon!" said the Little Duchess.

"Aaargh!" cried Gideon, as the Clockwork Duchess almost ran him down.

"I didn't know she could walk!" said Gideon. The Clockwork Duchess clanked the other way. She met a wall. "Charmed, I'm sure." *Clang,* her tin head bumped against it.

"What are those big bruises on your face?" asked the real Little Duchess.

"I fell over on the ice," lied Gideon. "I-I came to see if you were all right."

"I'm all right," lied Alice.

There was an awkward silence. *Clang!* The Clockwork Duchess head-butted another wall. But her perfect porcelain face showed no pain.

Then Alice burst out, "No, I'm not all right. I wish I was outside, ice sliding."

"The ice is melting," Gideon shrugged sadly.

"Well, I don't know then," said Alice, wildly. "Just doing anything! I'm going round the bend. Locked up in here, with her!"

"Charmed, I'm sure," wheezed the Clockwork Duchess as she came lurching by on stiff, tin legs.

Peep! A shrill whistle came from outside the room. But they couldn't hear it because of the creaks and whirrs from the Clockwork Duchess. She sounded like a walking scrapyard.

The cook made another urgent, *Peep!* Where was the boy? His five minutes were up. She peeked anxiously from the velvet curtains. She daren't whistle again. The Arch Duchess was sweeping down the corridor. She was heading for the Little Duchess's room.

"Do something!" the cook ordered herself.

She leapt out in front of the Arch Duchess. The cook was built like a rugby player. But the Arch Duchess had all the power.

"What is the meaning of this?" demanded the Arch Duchess, puffing herself up like an angry peacock. "Get out of my way!"

But the cook bravely blocked the corridor. The Arch Duchess kicked at her, with her sharp, pointy shoes. The

cook flinched. But she still stood, steady as a rock.

"How dare you!" fumed the Arch Duchess, her weasel eyes glittering.

The cook thought, "She's going to sack me, any second now."

"I was just going to see," said the cook, "if the Little Duchess wants any breakfast."

"She's not allowed breakfast!" spat the Arch Duchess. "She's being punished."

At that moment the smell of burning bread wafted up the stairs.

"Cook!" shrieked the Arch Duchess. "Is that my breakfast rolls burning?"

There was nothing else for it. The cook had to rescue the rolls. She rushed away, muttering rude words under her breath. Her mind was in turmoil. What would happen to the children now, with no one to protect them?

The Clockwork Duchess trundled to a halt. With a soft, groaning sound, she slumped forward from the waist, her arms dangling, and was silent.

An angry shriek came from outside, as the Arch Duchess hollered down the stairs. "And mind my teatime scones don't get scorched!"

"It's her," Alice hissed to Gideon, her eyes wide with horror.

"I'll hide," said Gideon.

"No time," said Alice. The key was already being rattled in the lock.

The Arch Duchess swept in, "Why was your door unlocked?" Then her eyes fell on Gideon. "What is he doing here?" she screeched. She turned and rushed out again.

"She's gone to fetch the guards!" said Gideon, his legs suddenly as weak as water.

He thought of all the crimes he could be charged with: thieving, trespassing, taking the Little Duchess out ice sliding. "They'll put me in chains," he groaned. "They'll lock me up for ever."

"No, they won't," said Alice. "Come on."

When the Arch Duchess came storming back with the guards, the

room was empty. "He was here!" she snarled.

The Sergeant clicked his heels and saluted. "Ma'am! Shall we send out search parties? We'll soon find the ruffian for you."

A furtive look crept over the Arch Duchess's face.

"Don't bother, Sergeant," she said. "I'll deal with this."

CHAPTER 10

Alice thought, "Thank goodness for this yellow rope."

She and Gideon were taking the cook's secret way out of the palace.

Plop. Plop. They could hear water dripping. Outside, the snow was thawing. Water was seeping down into the cellars.

Something flew past them on creaky wings. Gideon clasped the rope even tighter.

At last, they crawled through the iron grille.

Alice blinked, took a deep breath. "We're outside!"

The palace wall was behind them, the big, wide world in front. She lifted up her pale little face. Sunshine warmed it, like a blessing.

"You'd better go home," she told Gideon.

"I'm not going home," he said. "I'll just get another beating. I'm not going home ever again."

"Coooee!" called a voice.

They spun round. It was the faithful cook, charging through the palace gates. She'd rescued the breakfast rolls, then come rushing out to find them.

"You'd better run," she told Gideon. "This place will soon be swarming with guards. And you, milady, you must come back with me double quick. Old Prune-face is having hysterics. You'll only get yourself into more trouble."

But Alice didn't move. She was thinking, "The Arch Duchess will never let me out now. I'll be locked up forever with the Clockwork Duchess as my only friend."

"I'm not going back either," she told the cook.

"Milady!" said the cook, shocked. "What are you thinking of? You're a duchess. You have to go back."

"No, I don't," said Alice.

The cook knew that stubborn look, the way that the Little Duchess tilted her chin. She looked over her shoulder. Any second now, guards would come clanking out through the big iron gates.

Still the cook hesitated. She said, "What about the Grand Duke?"

"He won't even notice," sighed the Little Duchess.

The cook came to a decision. She plunged her hand into her apron pocket, gave something to Alice: "Take these." It was two bread rolls, still warm from the oven.

"Thank you," said Alice.

"It's not much," said the cook. "But it'll keep you both going until you find the fair."

"What fair?" asked Gideon.

"My brother, Captain Harper, owns a travelling fair. It was at Middleton, last I heard. Just tell him I sent you. He'll take you in. Now, hurry."

She watched them rush off.

"Follow the highway," she called after them. "And you can't miss Middleton. But keep out of sight.

103

They'll be looking for you."

"May they be safe," she whispered to herself. And wiped a tear from her eye.

But someone wasn't shedding tears. High up in the palace, the Arch Duchess was peering from Alice's window. She saw the Little Duchess vanish, with Gideon, into the trees.

"Good riddance," she thought. "That's all she's fit for. Running away with a ragged child. She was never a

proper duchess."

The Arch Duchess's dim but wily brain was busily plotting.

She'd been brought here, after her sister-in-law's death, to look after the Little Duchess. She hadn't had a bean before – she'd been a poor relation. But now she was used to a life of luxury, of ordering servants about. She didn't want to move back to her cold, draughty palace.

Should she tell the Grand Duke his daughter had run away?

"No point in bothering him with little details like that," the Arch Duchess schemed. "Not when there's another duchess to take her place."

This one would be much less trouble. All you had to do was oil her creaky joints every now and again.

The Grand Duke would never notice the difference. And, with a bit of cunning, no one else would either.

In fact, thought the Arch Duchess, this is a much better arrangement all round!

"We've got a proper duchess now," she told the Clockwork Duchess, as she started to wind her up.

CHAPTER 11

Gideon and Alice didn't know that there wasn't anybody chasing them. They ran as if demons were after them. There was no ice sliding now. The frozen roads and meadows were thawing. The grass was soggy, the lanes slushy. They only stopped for Alice to take off her heavy wig and struggle out of her Duchess dress.

"Now I can run like the wind," she said.

"Don't throw them away," said Gideon.

"Why not?"

"They're worth a lot of money. We could sell them."

"Oh," said Alice. Little Duchesses didn't have to think about money. "But you're not a duchess any more," she reminded herself. So she rolled up the frock, with the wig inside it, and strapped it on her back.

Little Duchesses didn't have to think about food, either. You rang a bell and servants rushed in and brought  you hot chocolate to drink in a china mug. Or made you a big fire so you could toast your toes.

"I'd like a mug of hot chocolate now," thought Alice. "And I'd like to be warm."

They had stopped after hours of tramping. Her feet ached, her toes were frozen, her silver slippers were soaked through. They'd eaten the bread rolls long ago. Now she was crouched in a field, her layers of petticoats all bedraggled, gnawing a frozen turnip. "I never dreamed I'd be doing this," she was thinking. Even the scarecrow looked surprised.

It wasn't even dark yet. But they couldn't go a step further.

"I've got blisters," said Gideon, rubbing his feet, "like pigeons' eggs." They rested in a ditch.

Alice was glad that she'd lugged the duchess dress with them. It made a good duvet. And the wig was a great hand-warmer. But she was still cold.

"How far to Middleton?" she asked Gideon, shivering. Whenever she'd travelled before, it was always by golden coach.

"I don't know," said Gideon. "Cook just said follow the highway."

An ice thief can stand the cold. But a little duchess isn't used to her toes turning blue and her belly growling.

"You shouldn't have come," said Gideon. He felt guilty now. Did she want to go back to the palace? Did she think she'd made a big mistake?

He daren't ask her in case she said. "Yes".

Instead, he said, "Watch this!" He tore off a grass stem, flattened it between his thumbs, then blew. It made a rude raspberry noise.

Alice's grave little face cracked into a grin.

"And watch this," said Gideon. He made a "Tsk, tsk" sound. "It doesn't always work," he warned her.

But it did work. Suddenly, a weasel shot its snake-like head up, watched them with its brilliant eyes, then popped down again.

"It's called weasel charming," said Gideon. "Try it. Just put your tongue behind your teeth.

Alice tried it, "Tsk, tsk, tsk. It's not working!"

"Look," whispered Gideon. The weasel had popped up somewhere else. Its bright, beady eyes were spying at them through the grass.

"Who does that remind you of?" said Gideon.

"The Arch Duchess!" This time, Alice laughed out loud.

And suddenly Alice didn't want to go back to her old life, to that chilly palace and that creepy clockwork friend you couldn't even share a joke with.

Even sleeping in a ditch was better.

"What's that noise?" said Gideon. He poked his tatty head out of the ditch.

It was coming from over the hill. There were drums beating, trumpets tooting. A boy passed, with a pig on a string.

"What's over that hill?" asked Gideon.

"It's Middleton, of course," said the boy, as if he was amazed they didn't know. "And the fair's there!" He sounded excited. "I'm taking our pig, to sell it."

Alice and Gideon crawled out of the ditch.

"What if the cook's wrong?" said Alice. "What if her brother turns us away?"

"Then we'll go somewhere else," said Gideon. But his eyes were anxious. He had no idea where somewhere else might be. He'd never been this far away from his village before. He'd never seen a fair before, either.

They came over the hill. There was Middleton below them, with the fair on the green. There were swarms of people, and sounds of music, and shouting: "Buy my fine gingerbread!" "Buy my sizzling hot sausages!"

Flags, red, green and yellow, decorated every stall.

They walked down the hill, their hearts fluttering like the flags.

"Where is Captain Harper?" demanded Alice. Without thinking, she'd put on her snootiest voice.

"Miss High-and-Mighty," laughed the girl she'd asked. "Dressed in dirty petticoats!"

They pushed their way through the crowds. Gideon's eyes were wide with wonder. There were fire-eaters,

tightrope walkers, tumblers...

"Aaaargh!" yelled Gideon as a huge man swished a cutlass over his head.

He was dressed as a pirate with an eyepatch and bristling red beard that spread out over his chest.

"Come and see our pirate play!" he boomed at them. "It has villains in it. And fighting. And fireworks! And it'll only cost you one penny!"

This time, Alice was careful not to sound snooty. She said, "Please sir, do you know Captain Harper?"

"Know him!" thundered the pirate. "I am him!"

He crouched down and pulled off his red false beard. "Now, what would two such ragged little ruffians want with the famous Captain Harper?"

CHAPTER 12

The fair was over. The people had all gone home. Only the fairground folk were left. They were crowding round Alice and Gideon. Some were in rainbow-coloured costumes with sequins. Some were dressed as fierce pirates with cutlasses. They looked curious. Some looked suspicious.

"These fairground folk are like my family!" boomed Captain Harper. "I would like to take you in. But they must agree."

The fairground folk murmured to each other. Alice thought anxiously, "What are they saying?"

"Well," demanded Captain Harper, "what is your verdict? My sister Peg has asked us to take them in. And, as you know, I would do anything for Peg."

"But they must earn their keep," said a fortune teller.

"They must," agreed Captain Harper. "For we cannot afford to feed them."

"What can they do?" asked a sausage seller. "Can they tumble or fire-eat? Can they juggle?"

Alice and Gideon looked hopelessly at each other.

"Can they tightrope walk?" asked a rope dancer. "Wheel a wheelbarrow with three dogs inside it and a duck on their heads?"

The fairground folk waited for their reply. Gideon searched frantically through his brain. He could steal ice. But winter was over – the ice had melted. He could charm weasels. But he didn't think anyone would pay to see that.

He was just thinking, "They aren't going to take us in. We'd better start walking," when Alice spoke up.

"I can do something," she said. "Just wait two minutes."

She hustled Gideon behind a gingerbread stall, then unstrapped the bundle from her back.

"What are you going to do?" Gideon asked, bewildered. She was fitting that heavy wig on again!

"I'm going to pretend to be the Little Duchess," hissed Alice.

"But you are—" began Gideon.

"But they don't know that. They just think I'm Alice."

"Oh," nodded Gideon. His face lit up with understanding. "That's a brilliant idea."

"Introduce me," said Alice, pushing him out from behind the stall.

"Err, errrr," stuttered Gideon, while the fairground folk waited.

"Lost your tongue, boy?" grinned a sword swallower.

Gideon took a deep breath.

"Ladies and gentlemen!" he said. "Here is a living, breathing likeness of our own Little Duchess! They look alike. They talk alike. They are as like as...as two peas in a pod!"

Alice came sweeping out from behind the stall, dressed in her fine

Duchess clothes. She had the haughtiest look on her face. She marched about, proud as a peacock. She stared down her nose at everyone, even the famous Captain Harper. Then said, in her best snooty voice, "Charmed, I'm sure!"

There was dead silence.

"Did they like it?" wondered Gideon.

Then Captain Harper laughed, a great, booming belly laugh. "Rat me!" he said. "It's uncanny. It could be the Little Duchess herself!"

Then everyone was laughing and clapping.

"Incredible! Even the Grand Duke couldn't tell the difference!"

"And have you no family?" asked a little dancer in a spangled tutu, wiping away a tear.

Alice and Gideon looked at each other. What should they say?

"No one to take care of you?" asked a tumbler.

That was much easier to answer. "No," Alice and Gideon said, together.

"Only Peg," added Gideon.

"Well, you have us now," roared Captain Harper, throwing his arms wide. "Welcome to your fairground family."

CHAPTER 13

"Roll up! Roll up, ladies and gentlemen!" yelled Gideon, beside their stall. He'd been shy at first. But now he'd taken to being a showman like a duck to water. "A penny to see the Little Duchess lookalike!"

They had travelled far and wide and, at each village they stopped in, people flocked to see Alice doing her Little Duchess act. Flouncing about with her nose in the air, fanning

herself and saying,
"Charmed, I'm sure."

Many people had
seen the Little Duchess
before, going past in her
golden coach. But even
those who'd never seen her
said, "It gives me the shivers! They're
the spitting image of each other!"

A boy passed and gave Gideon a
friendly greeting. "Hello, Gideon!" It
was Jem, the fire-eater's apprentice.

A motherly woman came by. It was
Maria, the fair's strongwoman. She
could carry four sheep at
once, two tucked under
each tree-trunk arm.
"Where's my Little
Duchess?" she said.

Alice poked her
head through the
curtains. "Here I am."

Maria gave them both a big bear hug, "You little darlings!"

"Phew," grinned Gideon as Maria stomped off. "She nearly squeezes the breath out of you!"

They'd been here no more than a month. But already Alice and Gideon felt they belonged. As if they'd been at the fair all their lives.

When they'd first arrived, Gideon often had nightmares. He'd see the red, roaring face of Pa in his dreams, feel a broom breaking on his back. But now he hardly had those bad dreams at all.

And Alice sometimes dreamed that her father the Grand Duke had moved heaven and earth to find her. That he came galloping up on his finest white horse and said, "Dear daughter, I've been looking for you everywhere."

But the truth was, no one was

searching. No one even seemed to know the Little Duchess was missing.

One day, after the show, Captain Harper came to see them. He looked worried, as if he had something difficult to say.

"I've been hearing whispers," he said.

Alice and Gideon looked at each other. Was there trouble coming? Just when they felt they were safe?

The Captain frowned, "Some people are saying you're the real Little Duchess."

Alice's heart give a sick lurch. She struggled to stay calm. "That's silly. Why are they saying that?"

"They say you're too much like her to be true! That you must be the real thing."

"But I'm not the Little Duchess," insisted Alice. She didn't feel as if she was lying. Those Little Duchess days seemed long ago. She was Alice now. She had a new life.

"She just looks like her, that's all," said Gideon.

"Hmmm." Captain Harper still looked unhappy. "They're even saying we kidnapped you. That under that Duchess frock, there are chains round your ankles."

"That's really stupid!" Gideon burst out.

"I know," said Captain Harper. "But it could mean trouble for us. Fairground folk have many enemies. They could try to close us down."

They stared miserably at each other.

"Does that mean you want us to go?" asked Alice.

"No, no, my dears," said the Captain. "We won't turn you out. We'll think of something—"

Jem hurried past. "The Grand Duke's coming by tomorrow. A whole mob of 'em, in their golden coaches. The Little Duchess will be with 'em."

Captain Harper sprang to his feet. "Couldn't be better!" he roared. "Now those whisperers will have to eat their words! Once they've seen the real Little Duchess, they'll stop spreading wicked rumours!"

That night, outside the big barn where the fairground folk slept, Gideon and Alice huddled close to the fire. Red sparks flew around them as they whispered.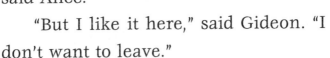

"We have to go," said Alice.

"But I like it here," said Gideon. "I don't want to leave."

"Neither do I. But what happens tomorrow when the coaches go past and there's no Little Duchess in them?"

Gideon shook his head. It would

only make the rumours stronger. What if Captain Harper was arrested for kidnapping? What if the fair was closed down?

What would happen to Maria and all the others?

"If they starve to death in a ditch it'll be all our fault!" said Alice.

Gideon gazed up at the starry sky. At the cold moon gazing down at them.

"We've got to go," agreed Gideon. "Later on tonight. When everyone's fast asleep."

CHAPTER 14

At midnight, with sad hearts, they crept out of the barn. Alice took the wig and Duchess dress. They were heavy to carry, but she couldn't leave them behind.

They tramped down muddy tracks in the moonlight.

"Where are we going?" asked Gideon.

"I don't know," said Alice.

When the dawn came up they

crouched in the dewy grass, chewing miserably on some bread and cheese. Alice remembered that first night after they'd run away, when they'd crouched in a muddy field, feeling just as miserable, munching turnips.

It didn't seem fair. They were homeless again, just when they'd found people they really liked and a place they felt they belonged.

Suddenly, the ground seemed to

shake. "What's that?" asked Alice, staring round.

They heard a loud rumbling sound like thunder.

"Hide!" said Gideon.

But there was no time. Six horses came galloping past pulling a golden coach. It was the Grand Duke! Going from one palace to another. People came out of their cottages to stare.

The Grand Duke sped past. Alice

didn't even catch sight of him; he was just a blur. For one mad moment she thought of running after the coach shouting, "Father, it's your lost daughter!" But he would only give her his cold, distant stare and say, "Daughter? What daughter?"

Another coach rumbled after him. Who was in it? It was the Arch Duchess. She peered out disdainfully. She saw the two children standing by the roadside. She didn't recognise either of them. Gideon didn't look like

the ragged boy she'd seen before. He had a fine, new crimson waistcoat and no bruises on his face. And Alice, without her duchess clothes, looked like any village child.

The Arch Duchess closed the curtains. "There's nothing interesting outside," she thought. She couldn't wait to get to the next palace.

The people waited. "Where's the Little Duchess's coach?" they said. Only Alice and Gideon knew it wasn't coming.

They'd already started walking, when they heard the blare of trumpets, the clashing of cymbals. Another golden coach came over the hill. It trundled much more slowly. It had to, so that the brass band marching beside it could keep up.

"It's the Little Duchess!" someone called out. The coach went past at walking pace. Everyone had time for a really good eyeball.

Gideon and Alice threw shocked glances at each other. They stared into the coach too.

She had her usual snooty face, stiff and cold as a stone mask. She stared straight ahead with empty cornflour-blue eyes.

"It's the Clockwork Duchess," hissed Gideon. "It's got to be!"

The Clockwork Duchess gave a jerky, royal wave.

"Charmed, I'm sure," she said, in her strange, wheezy voice. But nobody heard. Every sound she made was drowned out by the din of trumpets and cymbals. That was just what the Arch Duchess wanted.

The Clockwork Duchess was the perfect replacement. She caused no trouble. She never did anything unduchesslike. And if she got on your nerves you didn't wind her up.

But she had one big disadvantage. No matter how the Arch Duchess oiled her joints, she still couldn't stop them clanking. Every time the Clockwork Duchess waved to the peasants, her tin arm went, "Whirr, clank." Even peasants might get suspicious. But the brass band had solved that problem. When they travelled, the Arch Duchess wore earplugs, so she couldn't hear the racket.

The band hurried off at full toot, jogging behind the Clockwork Duchess's coach into the distance.

The villagers had a good gossip about them.

"I thought that pretend Little

Duchess at the fair might be real," said one. "But I was wrong. For there was the real Little Duchess, large as life!"

"And that pretend Little Duchess doesn't even look like her," said another. "What a swizzle. It wasn't worth a penny. For the real Little Duchess is much more beautiful."

"Yes!" added someone. "She has a prettier nose and bluer eyes and perfect skin. White as milk. With not a mark on it!"

"Aye, and the pretend Little Duchess has freckles. I shan't be paying to see her again. In fact, she's not like the real thing at all."

"Nothing like her," everyone

agreed angrily, as if they'd been cheated.

Alice and Gideon stared at each other. Gideon thought Alice might feel hurt. After all, they'd just said the Clockwork Duchess was more beautiful. But she seemed delighted. She gave Gideon a big grin.

"Don't you see?" she said. "We can go back to the fair! Now they think that they've seen the real Little Duchess all those whisperers will shut up. They'll stop saying I must be the real one. And that the fairground folk kidnapped me."

"You're right!" Gideon grinned back.

They began tramping back the way they'd come. But now their hearts were light. They laughed and joked on the way.

"Wait a minute," said Gideon, suddenly noticing something. "You're not carrying your wig, or your Duchess dress."

"I know," said Alice. "I left them behind in a ditch."

"Why?" said Gideon.

"Because I'm sick of the Little Duchess. I don't want to be her any more. And did you hear those people? No one will pay to see me anyway. Not now they think I'm nothing like the real thing."

"This is making my head ache," said Gideon. "What's real and what's not." But then it suddenly struck him – they had a serious problem.

"How are we going to make our living at the fair?" asked Gideon.

"I don't know," said Alice. That was worrying her too. "We'll just have to think of something."

CHAPTER 15

"Roll up! Roll up!" yelled Gideon.

Captain Harper came past, looking fierce in his pirate's outfit.

"Congratulations!" he boomed. "This new show of yours is a big hit. Look at the folk queueing to get in."

He swaggered away, swishing his cutlass.

Alice was behind the curtains of their stall, getting the show ready.

Gideon had taken his last penny.

He fastened his fat purse of money, then dashed inside to help.

The curtains opened. The crowd grew quiet.

"Welcome to the world-famous Weasel Circus," said Alice.

"Tsk, tsk, tsk," said Gideon.

Two weasel sisters flowed like orange snakes out of his pockets. He and Alice had charmed them from a rabbit burrow when they were babies. But they were like pets now, never shut up in cages. Every night they went out hunting. But they always came back.

"Ooooo!" went the audience as the weasel sisters jumped through hoops, pulled a miniature stage coach, and danced a minuet.

It's amazing what you can charm a weasel to do.

The audience were amazed too.

"Are those real weasels?" shouted a

small boy after the weasel sisters had taken a bow and dived back into Gideon's pocket. "Or are they clockwork?"

"Of course they're real," said his pa. "Anyone can see that."

"Bless the boy," explained his ma. "He's clockwork mad. He'll be saying the Little Duchess is clockwork next!"

Alice grinned at Gideon. He grinned back.

And everyone in the audience wondered what on earth they found so funny.

ORCHARD GREEN APPLES

HARDBACK

☐ Monkey-Man	Sandra Glover	1 84362 276 9
☐ The Ugly Great Giant	Malachy Doyle	1 84362 240 8
☐ Jalopy	Geraldine McCaughrean	1 84362 266 1
☐ Sugar-Bag Baby	Susan Gates	1 84362 070 7

ALL PRICED AT £8.99

PAPERBACK

☐ Monkey-Man	Sandra Glover	1 84362 278 5
☐ The Ugly Great Giant	Malachy Doyle	1 84362 241 6
☐ Jalopy	Geraldine McCaughrean	1 84362 267 X
☐ Sugar-Bag Baby	Susan Gates	1 84362 071 5

ALL PRICED AT £3.99

Orchard Green Apples are available from all good book shops,
or can be ordered direct from the publisher:
Orchard Books, PO BOX 29, Douglas IM99 1BQ
Credit card orders please telephone 01624 836000 or fax 01624 837033 or visit our
Internet site: www.wattspub.co.uk
or e-mail: bookshop@enterprise.net for details.

To order please quote title, author and ISBN
and your full name and address.
Cheques and postal orders should be made payable to 'Bookpost plc.'
Postage and packing is FREE within the UK
(overseas customers should add £1.00 per book).

Prices and availability are subject to change.